Old Moon

Volume 1: Summer 2022

Contents

Published by Old Moon Quarterly.

Each author retains the copyright to their story.

Cover art by Caitlyn E. Camp.

The collection and arrangement © 2022 Old Moon Quarterly.

A Town Called Trepidation

By Paula Hammond

Firepoint chewed the nub of her cigar and stared into the wind. She'd let the tobacco burn out hours ago, afraid the embers would give her position away. Still, there was something oddly comforting about the little damp stub of Old Egyptian. A taste of home in these faraway lands.

The sun had already set, but the tiny quartz crystals that littered the White Sands would glow for many hours yet, giving off just enough ambient light to make camp without the need of a fey-lamp. Just as well, as tonight she hadn't the patience to perform the rituals. Besides, it would disturb Apophis and he needed a good night's rest. Pepper dragons made hardy mounts but were notoriously irritable when tired.

"Not long now, old boy," she growled, running her hand through the soft spikes that covered Apophis' head. "Soon be there."

Trepidation wasn't much of a town but she and Apophis knew it well. It was just a few hour's ride from the border, and a natural stopping-point for travellers heading north into the Glittering Lands of Ni' Hodisǫs. If the Winter twins had pulled ahead of them, then Trepidation was where they'd be.

Logic dictated they should press on, but she'd been tracking the twins for a week solid, and ten days in the saddle was just about eight days too long. She was so tired that even a well-sprung bed and bottle of cactus wine didn't seem that enticing. "Besides," she mumbled, half to Apophis, half to herself, "I could be chasing ghosts."

Truth be told, she'd been trailing nothing but dust and coffee-fumes for days. Instinct told her she was on the right track. It wasn't much. But it would have to do.

****

It was cold now. Wind flowed fast and chill in these low lands. Without a fire, she and Apophis would need extra layers to get them through the night. Luckily blankets, stashed in the saddle bags, accounted for the bulk of their gear. And while their flamboyant Mayan glyphs were meaningless, their weight more than made up for the lack of any warming enchantments.

It was as she was pulling the heavy weave across the pepper dragon's back that she saw the first flash of tracer fire. Startling blue streaks, arcing across the horizon, followed by the low earthquake-thrump of heavy ammunition. A sure sign of alchemy at work.

Firepoint had seen long-guns and mortar at the battle of Neter-khertet when two navies had fought themselves bloody over a spit of uninhabitable land named for the Egyptian afterworld. So far, she'd never encountered them on land. Never in the home of the Ni' Hodisǫs. This could only mean one thing: war.

"Neck!" she swore wearily. Pharaoh's conflict with the Eceni was raging all across the Great Ocean, but she'd no idea that the kingdoms of the New World had been dragged into the madness. This would not end well. Not for Egypt. Not for the Eceni. And not for anyone caught in the middle of the whole crazy mess.

****

Firepoint had been named for the great Pharos lighthouse in the land of her birth. Her father's ancestors had fought beside Cleopatra when the legendary Pharaoh had won her victory against the Roman scourge. But, through her mother's line, she was descended from the flame-haired Ecini who had broken Rome's grip in the West and chased Suetonius Paulinus all the way to the Baltic. She was born to war, of warrior stock, but this felt too damn close to home.

Everyone knew the Eceni had gold-fever. It was just a matter of time before they tried to lay claim to these New World riches. Pharaoh would use that as an excuse to strengthen his own presence in the region. It was a damnable mess. The politics of it didn't overly concern her but, as a child of both worlds, it was just a matter of time before she'd be asked to choose a side. And all Firepoint really wanted was to be left alone to collect her bounties.

Settling down beside Apophis, she uncorked a hinu of bread-ale, savouring the warming taste of ginger and mandrake, before once again unrolling the wanted poster.

The hieroglyphs lacked the elegance of classic Kemet script but were easy enough to read: "Wanted for Sacrilege Most Severe." No details were given beyond the requirement that the felons must be returned alive. That meant they'd stolen something from the one of the temple complexes, and would be sacrificed in a way that was neither clean nor quick. Payment, as was usual for such bounties, was mostly symbolic. Jade, salt, quetzal feathers.

Real money would be made trading the jade and feathers with the Inupiat healers in the frozen North. Thoth alone knew what they used them for. She'd heard rumours, of course. Tales of ice magic and undead servitors crafted from seal blubber and blood. Stories of skin-switchers and killing spirits. Tales of wild women riding the aurora winds and emerging impossibly young and alluring. But, then, these lands held so many wonders. Who knew what was true and what was wishful thinking?

****

She didn't remember falling asleep but awoke with a jolt. The air was crisp enough to tell her she'd slept for many hours but the glow on the horizon wasn't that of approaching dawn. Trepidation was burning.

"Neck!" Firepoint spat in frustration. 'Ok, boy," she grumbled, clambering to her feet and hauling the blanket from Apophis' back. "Wake up. Looks like morning's come early."

Apophis was a light sleeper and Firepoint knew that whatever had woken her would have awoken the dragon too. She also knew that the great lizard would lie there, feigning sleep, until he was presented with his ration of 'gator meat. Then, he'd turn his opalescent eyes on her, yawn lazily, and try his very best to go back to sleep. Damn shiftless dragon. Some days she wished she could afford to hire a sky barge. "Ah, but where would the fun be in that be, ay?" she asked, ruffling Apophis' feathers absent-mindedly. "Come on boy, shake your hide, no games today. Trouble's brewing and I have a feeling it's got our name written all over it."

Dragon riding wasn't for the faint-hearted. The beasts yawled like sailboats but if you knew how to sit—legs wrapped around the saddle post—then you quickly shook off the motion-sickness. If there was a way to stop the saddle sores, she was yet to find out.

By the time the sun was up, there was no missing it. Smoke palled above Trepidation like a purpling bruise. This time it wasn't military ordnance. No, this didn't have the look or stink of Pharaoh's khēmia. But a couple of albino outlaws with a fondness for explosions might just make this sort of mess.

"The bank," Firepoint groaned. A high-value target with little or no security. The grain bank was exactly the sort of mark the Winter twins loved. So much for ghosts.

Firepoint tapped her heels into her mount's hide, and gave a throaty hearty "Hua!"—the signal for Apophis to pick up speed. The dragon yowled in reply and the White Sands became whirling dust beneath his splayed feet. Desert became scrub, and the town soon roared into focus.

****

For the most part, Trepidation was no different from any other frontier town. Quiet, except on market day. Peaceful, except on payday. The people, just passing through. When asked, even those who'd lived there their whole lives would stare at the malachite-tinged horizon and talk about how they ought to be moving on. And like any frontier town, it had just one street. A street that was now buzzing with townsfolk.

The grain bank sat on the corner. The first or last building you'd see depending on which direction the trail was taking you. It had been an imposing building. One of the few in these parts built from stone, it was twice as high as any surrounding structure.

Firepoint left Apophis at the hitching post and shouldered her way through the crowd. Most were just curious but, directly in front of the bank's scorched frontage, she could see a line of militia hunkered behind a makeshift barricade, black-powder fire sticks primed and ready.

The bank doors still clung to their hinges, the bottom half blackened and buckled, the top shattered like splintered golem teeth. Behind them, Firepoint could see flashes of bone-white and silver: the Winter twins.

She picked out the militia leader by his look of ragged frustration. "Got a bounty on these two," she started without introduction, "what's the story?"

Firepoint wore her affiliations boldly. The travel-worn leathers and desert grime of the bounty hunter. The shaven head of the Egyptian priestly class. The body ink of the Ecini—a knot of impossible animals

9

etched in soot that ran from her left cheek, down her neck, to her finger tips. To most folk she looked exactly what she was: an itinerant mongrel, a very long way from home.

The man she addressed noted all of these things but it was as his eyes lighted on her lapis-encrusted wrist bands that his attitude changed from indifference to deference. He'd never seen a theurgist in the flesh before.

Protocol kicked in: "From Father Sun and Mother Earth I welcome you with open heart and open hearth." The man rattled out the universal greeting with the air of one who had better things to do, then added, as an afterthought, "I'm Water's Edge. Pleased to get whatever help I can. I'm in a mess here and that's the truth of it."

Firepoint returned the greeting, scanning the building curiously, as Water's Edge related the morning's events.

"They blew the vault just before dawn. Blew the door, then set fire to the stables on the way out of town. Probably to slow down any pursuers. Pure chance we ran into them. We were coming. They were going. Things happened pretty fast after that. They hightailed back to the vault. Barricaded themselves in. That was a couple of hours ago. It's been a stand off ever since."

Firepoint took in the scene. Groggy-looking guards, bandaged and bloody. A pair of scrawny little camels tethered out back. There were no wagons. None of those little curly-haired Lakota horses to pull them. How the hell did they expect to move the grain? No, Firepoint thought, this whole thing stinks. Why blow the vault? With the guards out of action, they could have forced the doors. Carried away a wagon-load of grain and been away before dawn. They'd get a fair price in any settlement town, no questions asked. Why draw attention to themselves?

"Anyone know you were coming to town?" she ventured.

Water's Edge shrugged. "We make our rounds regular. Aim to be here every new moon when the courts sit and they need extra security. It's no secret."

"So maybe the Winter twins knew you'd be here. Probably didn't plan on getting caught but maybe it wouldn't hurt if you'd have given chase a-while. Would have looked good. Like you'd foiled the robbery. Then... then..."

Firepoint ran the permutations. New moon coming, a robbery thwarted, a cause for celebration. She was prepared to guess that when the grain was checked it would have been laced with something nasty. Deadly? Not the twins' style, but knocking out a whole town while they looted the place bare, that would fit. "Yes," she said to no-one in particular, "the offence is grave. The cause is true."

Firepoint had a habit, born from solitude, of speaking her thoughts aloud. Luckily Water's Edge was a man whose livelihood relied on paying attention. At her words, he blanched and started barking his men back from the barricade. He didn't think they were in any real danger, but magic wasn't a thing you took chances with.

****

Magic, theurgisty, relied on the good will of the gods. A sorcerer channelled their grace. Although Firepont was an acolyte of Thoth, the seven great civilizations shared many common beliefs. Father Sun and Mother Earth were widely worshipped, alongside a wealth of local gods and goddesses who protected hearth and home, under a variety of local names. They would assist only if the offence was grave, the cause was true. Firepoint's words were both an invocation and an invitation. She was asking the gods for help.

Time to go to work.

With a shrug, Firepoint threw off her voluminous dust-coat and hide-bound boots to reveal a carnelian shendyt kilt and tunic. To outsiders the clothes merely looked exotic, but to a fellow adept, every piece told its own story. Her wrist bands would focus and ground her power. Tucked in her sash was a heavy apotropaic wand which would give her protection, both physical and spiritual. It was a wicked-looking thing, with a blade that curved along her thigh, its hippo-tusk hilt tucked into a scarlet sash. The steel had been quenched with her own blood and etched with her true name, making it impossible for anyone else to wield it. Around her neck, and on her fingers she wore charms, crafted from horn, hair, and electrum. These were designs of her own devising, and wove together Eceni and Egyptian glyphs in a way that both cultures found disturbing.

With a practiced motion, she traced a circle in the sand with a bare foot, then stepped inside its protective lines.

As a theurgist of the third degree, she could forgo the ritual cleansing but the gods still expected a degree of reverence. An amulet bag around her neck would furnish all that was necessary: shavings from the skull of a dead man, the needles from a silver fir, myrrh, frankincense, and styrax resin. Dropped in the centre of the circle, it caught fire the moment it touched the sacred earth, filling the air with fragrant smoke that curled itself around Firepont's out-stretched arms like a pair of golden shackles.

Somewhere someone was shooting. Firepoint was vaguely aware of the bobbing heads of the Winter twins, the stench of black powder. Shots were returned, curses exchanged. A burning pain in her side told her she'd been hit, but that was no matter. She was no longer on this plane. Already her ka was communing with the gods, receiving the words she needed to begin weaving the spell.

****

While Father Sun gave Firepoint the words, Mother Earth gave her the power. It was a power unique to her, fueled by the blood of her ancestors. It roared through her, channelled by the touch of bare feet to bare earth—invisible but tangible. As it did so, Firepoint smelt moss, freshly-tilled soil, the musk of deer. Felt the presence of beings old and unknowable.

Head thrown back, tattoos blazing Firepoint opened her mouth and spoke. The creature who used her lips sounded neither male nor female. Nor was it a beast that any listener would have recognized. It made a snarl of pure, primal fury before it slowly, deliberately, began crafting words. They echoed jarringly, as though spoken from a great distance by something unused to human anatomy. At the same time,

the earth began to ripple like something beneath the surface was
clawing its way towards the grain bank.

Had Firepoint been aware of her surroundings she would have seen
the Winter twins racing to scramble over the ravaged door with the
look of one being chased by Anubis himself. She would have seen the
militia swear and drop their guns. She would have seen the townsfolk
howl and run. But, at that moment, she saw nothing beyond the
shadow realm where the gods held court with mortals foolish enough
to seek them out.

The twins had just reached the barricade when Firepoint finally
opened her strange green eyes. Everything stopped as though, with one
look alone, Thoth's greatest sorcerer could halt time itself. Maybe she
could. Or maybe it was merely the curiousness of the scene that
stopped the thieves in their tracks.

For a moment they regarded one another. The twins, dressed in
black—pale, pink-eyed, and cocky. Firepoint, tall and wiry as a
willow—a study in poise and suppressed fury. Then, the albinos
seemed to shake off their torpor. As one, they raised their fire sticks.
Hammers fell, flints sparked, guns belched. At the same time,
Firepoint brought her arms together, straining against the gold shackles
as though they were real and not crafted from mist. Where the bands
met, a serpent of light began to grow. It hit the hunks of lead propelled
from the duo's guns with a sizzle. They dropped to ground inches
away from Firepoint, as molten as the day they were first cast.

The light rolled on, hissing and boiling, turning the ground white
hot. Finally light met flesh, the serpent reared like a golden uraeus and

struck. The twins gasped and fell to their knees, as the mouth of the royal cobra opened to swallow them.

Only it didn't devour them. As the uraeus bore down on the cowering figures, they began to shrink. Smaller and smaller, denser and denser, until they resembled little more than tiny clay statues caught by a potter in a moment of abject terror.

Firepoint lowered her arms, blinking like a sleeper awakened, and stepped out of the circle to where the tiny ushabti lay. "Less trouble on the trail this way," she said with a grim smile.

As she stooped, she noticed the wound on her side for the first time, and gave quiet hiss of pain. The bullet had seared her flesh and clipped her ribs but a probing finger told her it was a clean wound. It would have to be attended to—but first thing's first.

Whistling to Apophis to follow, Firepoint turned on her heels and headed off towards Mother Haloke's boarding house. With an amazed splutter, Water's Edge gathered up her discarded clothes and fell clumsily into step. "So, what now?" he asked in a tone of barely suppressed excitement.

"Hot bath, bowl of sumac soup and, if you're in the mood, the tavern has some fine ale. Egyptian. Expensive imported stuff. You're buying."

She didn't wait to see if he replied.

Stella Splendens

By Graham Thomas Wilcox

They buried my father in our tombs of yore. A Mass was recited thereafter, and it did him little justice.

The priest preached. He knew his audience. Knights, and the children of knights. He stood at the altar, speaking blood and thunder. That altar was a relic of our house, wrought in silver and wood, stained dark by the ages. The work of Flanders, perhaps, or else those Italian cities that yet swear to the Imperial eagle. It was a grotesque of the old tradition, carved in the shape of flayed corpses, their backs bent beneath a tomb, their faces upturned and yearning.

The sermon spoke of Christ. His cross, his death, his love. Oh, how he adored war and warmakers. The blood of martyrs, the wine of heroes, so on and so forth. Christ as the knight-king of all Christendom, crowned in iron with a smoking sword.

I found I could picture only his tomb, empty as the Emperor's throne but for the scent of hallowed blood. But for the earth, wet and churned.

My mind wandered. My eyes prickled with sights.

****

Corpses, bereft of skin, trudged beneath an errant moon. They dripped with thorns. Winged babes sang old marching songs, mouths slack, eyes vacant. I walked alongside them, weeping blood. We came to a keep, strong-walled and tall. Cages hung from its towers. They held age-browned bones in white surcoats, and they rattled in the breeze.

I knew this place. Grosz, the Poles called it. We knew it as Pfennig. A dollop of wood and stone on the Baltic coast, much lashed by wind and wave. I fought a single combat outside its gate two winters ago. It was daylight then, I recall, a rare day of high sun amid the snow. But now, I saw it as night. No stars salted the sky, but the moon burned near, so very near, silvering the seafoam with its glow.

We besieged the keep alongside the German Order. It could not hold. The occupants knew as much and would surrender. Honour alone delayed them.

The castellan was an old man, but chivalrous. He would have ridden out himself, lonesome but for a lance, had he not lost a leg three years past. His son came out in his stead, proud and high-helmed below the crescent moon.

Father led our banner. A dozen lances constituted the entire might of our house. I was no knight then, and so served Father in his lance. He owned a knight's name, did Father, and would have sat this Polish sprat down hard. He petitioned the German Order, and their marshal granted us the right of single combat. Father in turn conferred that right to me.

I stood across from the Polish man-at-arms. Unknighted, as myself. Perhaps why Father deferred his death to me. But I thought not.

I did not look back at our lines. I knew what I would see. Chaplains swinging censers and monks chanting a dirge. Men, beards stiff with frosted snot, scourging themselves bloody and crying out to God. I did not look back.

But I knew Father watched. The last I saw him, the moon wrought eldritch angles of his face. His mouth and eyes were deep pits. Tombs.

He said he loved me as he clapped the sword into my hand. My harness was bright and clean. The rivets shone like eyes in the night.

The Pole. Mieszko was his name, I think. It shames me that I cannot remember it well. I remember his armour though. A new bascinet, with the long-snooted visor popular among the Franks and the Englishers. A coat-of-plates in his family's colours: a quartered field of *gules* and *argent*, a bleeding stag their crest. Everything polished to the mirror. It was something from a chanson.

The ground was too soft for horses. We dismounted. We saluted. Trumpets blared over the chanting monks and we set upon one another, weapons held at half-swords.

Measure means less in armour. You will not die from a single stroke, most like, and so you may draw closer. This meant I could smell the wine and onions on his breath when he threw the first swing. A mordschlag, his sword gripped by the blade and hefted as a hammer. I caught it on my blade between my hands, wrenched it down, thrust up at his visor. He voided my thrust, returned his own.

Fast, fast. The devil's own tongue, that blade of his. He screeched a furrow across my helm, and then another. I feinted high, then thrust low. He dipped, took the blow on his armour, swung another mordschlag. I parried, but it had been a feint. He stepped around me, sought an angle for his thrust, found it and let fly. I turned and staggered from this one, felt it ping off my spaulder like a dragon's tail.

He was good. Better than I. I would die here, in front of God and Father and those cross-humping monk-knights. The injustice appalled me.

I advanced, beat his point with my own, switched grips smooth as you please and hewed a mordschlag to his knee. A favoured play of mine, much practised in the tiltyard. He swatted it aside all the same, bound my blade with his and walked me down.

Death, sang the waves. *Death*, laughed the moon.

He cleared my sword and thrust into my armpit, straight through maille and gambeson. A clean blow. A killing blow, more times than not. I felt his blade puncture my flesh, hot as nails in hell. It drove far, but not far enough. It stuck fast when he tried to withdraw. Caught on sundered rings and torn linen.

I heard Father then, clarion-clear.

"Kill him, boy! Kill him!"

Let no man claim I am not a dutiful son. Gripping my sword by hilt and blade, I got it behind the Pole's helm, wrenched him forward, broke his posture, then ripped him to the ground. He landed facedown at my feet.

He almost struggled up on his elbows before my knee crushed him back down into the icy mud. I drew my dagger, groped for his visor, turned it to one side and dragged it open. I pried the dagger through his teeth into his mouth. Up, up, and up further still until it clicked against the top of his brainpan. His sword yet dangled under my arm and in my side, bouncing with every movement. He twitched and struggled, but I knew he was dead when I smelled shit.

Knights and monks surrounded me. Corpses, I saw, corpses all, dancing their victory at night by the sea.

"*Deo volente*," they cheered. They brandished crosses, waved swords. Scourges whacked bones and musty flesh. Their brothers in the cages on the castle wall rose and jigged in sympathy.

I wept warm tears of blood and embraced my father. His face was flat and dim. His mouth yawed wide and wider, a great dark cavern. It looked wet. All the absent stars flowed forth.

The Questing Beast

By Carys Crossen

My antecedents are unfortunate, it is true (*diabolical!* **Shameful!**
Malignant!) But the blame cannot be heaped upon my feline shoulders.
My mother was out walking in the woods one day and encountered a
handsome gentleman with a tongue that could have parted the thighs
of Lucrese. (**With flattery**). Yes, I am sure they know what I meant.

If he been merely a handsome gentleman, then I would not be here
telling you this story. But Mother caught a glimpse of him in the
stream they stood by, and it revealed his true nature to her (*he was a
demon*. **Bad.** Wicked).

Not that his being a demon worried Mother. In fact, she found it
quite exciting (*or so Father told us later*). They fell to on the
riverbank, and I (*I*, **I**, I, we) was the result of that brief coupling. Once
our fame had grown enough for people to gossip about us, some said
Mother lusted after her brother, and she bargained with a demon for
his love, (**arrant nonsense!**) which is ludicrous. Mother had only one
brother and he coughed himself to death in his thirteenth year. (She
slept with Father because she wanted to).

Forgive the constant interruptions. My nature is a divided (*shared*)
one. I have the head and neck of some enormous serpent, and my cool
snake's brain has sway over my being for most of the time. But my
shoulders and trunk are those of a leopard (*disdainful*), my haunches
those of a lion (**vain**) and my feet are stag's hooves (skittish). My

21

jumble of features is never quite in accord, but we manage well enough (*true,* **true**, <u>true,</u> *we are most wise and cunning and courageous*).

My (**our**) – very well, *our* mother's hellish fetish found her out at our birth. She never thought to conceal her pregnancy, despite her pointed lack of a husband *(little fool!)* Yes, I will concur with that sentiment. So, I – we, my apologies – were born, with a voice like a pack of baying hounds <u>(ironic)</u>. Yes, ironic. Happily, the midwives were so stunned by our appearance that they quite failed to kill me (*us*) and I – we – made our way to the sanctuary of the forest on shaking lion and leopard legs and deer hooves.

Mother got burned at the stake (**a bad death**). Forgive me if we are unemotional, it is the snake in us. Besides, we never knew Mother. I – the snake's head, I – learned all this long after the event.

We slunk off to the forest, where we were quite at home and where we found sanctuary <u>(for a short while)</u>. We loved the quiet forests, the peaceful hills, and encountered not a soul. Then the hunters came.

News of our birth spread, and the hunters followed apace. Some were, we admit, justifiably annoyed *(we soon developed a liking for sheep and pigs)*. Others wanted the fame our death would bring (**vain wretches!**), others fancied themselves virtuous and meant to rid the land of our evil (**puffed-up brats!**) We are cunning, and evaded the hunters, or the leopard and the deer in us did (*it was a nuisance!* <u>Lonely</u>). Yes, it was a little lonely, but we prefer the solitary life.

(*We met Father once*). Yes, so we did. He was pleasant enough, though shifty and duplicitous. Our desire for a quiet life is the one thing we are all in agreement about (**yes, peace.** <u>Stillness and silence</u>). Father prefers to cause a ruckus. The only reason he visited us at all is that Sir Pellinore was pursuing us at the time and Father wanted to play with him.

Pellinore was the most persistent of the many who hunted us. He was a mediocre knight by the standards of Camelot, the greatest kingdom in the world. He was well-meaning (*a decent fighter.* **Honest.** <u>Kindly</u>). Any other kingdom would have considered it a boon to have him in its service.

But not Camelot. Camelot, under the reign of King Arthur, was overflowing with greatness. The King himself (**the most valiant in the land!**), the magician Merlin <u>(wise beyond compare)</u>, and the company of the Round Table. There was Sir Bors, who had the strength of ten men, Sir Gawain *(cunning!)* whose trickster nature concealed a heart of great courage and integrity, Sir Galahad, pure and chivalrous *(a bit self-righteous, if you ask us)*. And many, many more.

(**Like Sir Lancelot**). Ugh, why must you always dredge up Lancelot? The lion in me adored him, but I, the snake, perceive things differently, and to my black unblinking eyes there was nothing in him but spectacular good looks and arrogance. Besides, he was covetous (*greedy.* <u>Selfish</u>). Show him a woman with a ring on her third finger of her left hand and he wouldn't rest until he bedded her.

But to return to Sir Pellinore. He had taken it upon himself to hunt and kill us, partly as a demonstration of his knightly prowess, partly because we had been eating someone else's sheep (**excellent mutton**). The sheep belonged to a poor shepherd, and their loss would not have troubled most of Camelot's knights – there is not much glory to be found in chasing after mutton stealers.

But Pellinore was kindly disposed towards peasants and beggars and orphans and the like (compassionate. *A soft touch*). When the shepherd came to beg for assistance, Pellinore volunteered to help, and Arthur agreed. The king apparently suggested Lancelot accompany Pellinore, but Lancelot had already promised his services to Queen Guinevere, escorting her to visit the King and Queen of Orkney.

(A good thing, or we would not be here telling this tale). Yes, yes, I'm getting to that. Pellinore was an accomplished woodsman and tracker, we will admit that, and once he had our trail we had to flee for our life. Killing Pellinore was not an option, although the leopard in us longed to rip out his throat *(pounce, grab, close jaws, end of)*. Yes, but killing a knight of Camelot would have brought every other knight down upon our snakish head, and we would never have known peace again (**true, our serpent head is wise**).

So, things dragged on for a fortnight or so. Always we kept one step ahead of Pellinore, but no further. And he was dogged, determined, inexorable in his pursuit. His knightly honour was at stake.

We were getting quite worn down and dispirited when Father found us. *(We didn't know it was Father at first)*. He was disguised, you see, as a wounded doe. We tried to take a bite out of her, and she promptly turned into a handsome man and rapped our snout (*that was cheating.* **Dishonourable**). It was Father, of course he cheated. Now be silent for a little while and let me continue (*apologies.* **Carry on**).

Thank you. Father introduced himself and explained what he wanted, all in the same breath. He wanted to corrupt Pellinore, as a challenge to himself. We queried why he didn't try the marvellously virtuous and gallant Galahad if he wanted a true challenge, and he explained, but we didn't quite understand. (He said a fanatic latches on to one pole of morality as easily as the other and turning them around was no great labour). That was our deer self. It is silent most of the time, but it does seem to understand a great deal more than our other parts.

But to return to Father. He thought Pellinore would be a good challenge, as those thoroughly decent types are harder to seduce into evil than most humans. And he said if we assisted him, he'd make sure Pellinore would pursue us no longer.

We had doubts, of course. There was something uncanny about Father. (It was the eyes). It was. His eyes had a way of looking past you, as though you were distracting him from something much more important. *(But we had few choices left)*.

So of course, we agreed to do as Father instructed us.

In retrospect, perhaps we are no wiser than Mother was.

****

Father informed us we needed bait, to lure in Pellinore. Not sheep – Father always liked to play with high stakes.

We went to the nearest village and snatched a child, as Father had bid us do. A little girl, with black hair and freckles on her nose. *(The village women nearly killed us).* Yes, those women were fearsome. We (foolishly) assumed the loutish youths scrapping on the village green would be the biggest threat, but they all screamed and fled when they saw us coming (**milk-and-water weaklings!**)

The village women were not nearly so meek. They chased us, screaming vengeance and waving knives and broomsticks, all the way back to the forest, where we managed to lose them in the trees. (**Father thought it was funny**). Yes, he was highly amused and that was when we first began to have doubts about his plan.

We didn't hurt the little girl. We only wanted to use her as bait – well, Father did. He told us to wait until he came back with Pellinore. We curled up around her to make sure she didn't run away and waited.

It was tiresome, waiting. (The child's sobs were very unpleasant). So they were. We had no desire to harm anyone, not really. We only wanted to live in peace, and we were not sure how kidnapping this child would aid our desires. (*Father had promised. We kept telling ourselves that).* So we did, until someone – I think it was our deer self – pointed out that Father was a demon, and so his word was not to be trusted.

I think that was when we decided not to wait any longer, but to go and find out exactly what Father was up to.

We had to wait a while longer for the girl to finish crying. We tried to speak to her, but she only wailed harder *(our voice is not soothing).* Eventually she exhausted herself and stopped sobbing, and we told her we meant her no harm and if she would be quiet, we would go and explore.

So off we went, the girl riding on our back and looking much happier. It took us a little time to find Father, but the leopard in us is an expert tracker *(even a demon leaves subtle signs)*. We found Father amid a circle of standing stones, having an intense conversation with a pale, resolute-looking Pellinore.

The girl and we kept silent and peered at the scene from behind one of the great stones thrusting towards the sky.

"It's the only way," Father was purring, eyes flicking up and down Pellinore as though he wanted to gobble him up. "The Questing Beast is devious beyond all measure. That child will surely perish if you do not agree to my terms. Your service, your being, in exchange for the child's safe return and the power to kill the Beast."

Pellinore was reluctant, we could tell. (Wise man). But we were confused by Father's words. It was not what we had agreed. And what was this Questing Beast?

"What is the Questing Beast?" we whispered – or what passes for a whisper in our voice. We were lucky Father did not hear.

But the little girl did.

"I think he means *you*," she hissed in where my ear would be if my head were not a snake's head.

Her words took a few moments for my normally quick intellect to comprehend, but once they penetrated the fog of Father's deception I was enraged. That is, *we* were enraged. The lion and leopard in us were roaring their fury and even our timid deer self was filled with ire and longed to charge Father with lowered antlers (if we had antlers).

"Come with us!" we said to the girl, and we strode forth from our hiding place.

"Father!" we roared. "You double-crossing scoundrel!"

The expression on Father's face – oh, we shall remember it until the day we die! It was a priceless mix of outrage, shock and pure annoyance. Pellinore turned white as salt, but he drew his sword, nonetheless.

"You said if we lured in Pellinore you'd deal with him and let us live in peace! You said nothing about our getting killed!" we shouted. Father was totally unabashed, of course. He recovered from his shock and only smirked.

Pellinore was hovering nearby, his gaze flicking from Father to us. We realised quickly that only surprise was keeping him in suspense, and that the sooner we gave him something else to consider the better. We turned to the girl.

"Run to the knight!" we told her, and so she did.

"Take the girl!" we roared at Pellinore, and to his credit he scooped her up and ran for the edge of the woods. (**Father got angry when we did that**).

Yes, he was most infuriated. He shouted at Pellinore to come back, that only he could give Pellinore the power to kill the Questing Beast, but Pellinore ignored him (sensible man). Then Father turned his rage on *us*, and we felt the full fire of a demon's fury.

For the first time, we glimpsed his true form.

(Do not ask us to describe it!) Hush now! His form defied true description in any case. It was not grand, or terrifying, or even

unnatural. We can only describe him as a decrepit, broken-down, starved reckling. (**What could Mother have been thinking?**) Perhaps he was better-looking when Mother met him. But when we beheld him, we saw a man's shape, twisted by suffering, haggard and wretched, with a few stray bedraggled feathers drifting at its back.

(But strong. So, so strong). Yes, for all his miserable appearance, Father was a demon and had the powers of Hell at his command.

(Luckily, we are half-demon ourselves). Yes, I think Father had forgotten about that. And so there we both were, locked in combat at the standing stones.

To this day, our four selves can recall little about that fight. To my snake's mind, it is a jumble of images and slashes of pain and spikes of triumph as we land a blow (*biting Father's leg, striking him with our paw,* **he raking his claws down our side**, *blood – not sure whose,* **the sound of our voice**, his shrieks, all muddled together). We cannot recall how we came to be lying on the ground, utterly spent and with knives sticking in us every time we moved. But we recall Father standing over us, livid, about to deal a death blow.

And we remember Pellinore hurling himself upon Father, driving him back, and the slash of his sword that severed Father's left hand from his arm.

Then we recall only Father's howls of agony, a sound like a thunderclap and Father disappearing (**a coward at heart**). Then the dark.

****

When we came to, it was to find Sir Pellinore and the little girl staring down at us. Pellinore still had his sword drawn but had refrained from using it while we were unconscious (**honourable.** *Foolish.* <u>Both</u>).

"If you mean to kill us, please make it swift," we groaned.

"Don't kill it!" piped up the little girl. "It's a nice monster."

Pellinore groaned, rubbing at his eyes in weary fashion.

"I'll never get things sorted out here," he grumbled.

But he did eventually, and even somewhat to his *(our)* satisfaction. Pellinore asked us for the full story, and we explained about wanting peace and meeting Father and our (**ill-advised**) bargain. He was angry about our kidnapping the little girl <u>(Margery)</u>. Yes, Margery, and we conceded that had been a wicked action, but we had not hurt her, nor had we intended to *(despite what Father had claimed)*.

To conclude, we convinced Pellinore that despite our origins and our recent doings we were not an evil creature *(just a bit…problematic)*. And he acknowledged that despite our theft of the sheep, we had never truly harmed anyone. (**And we saved him from having to sell his soul.** <u>He was most grateful for that</u>). As he should have been.

Our little conference ended in another bargain. Unlike the one with Father, everyone gained something of value *(the best kind of bargain!)*

Pellinore returned Margery to her family, where, due to her fortunate rescue, she became a kind of good-luck charm to her people and lived a happy and prosperous life. Pellinore returned to Camelot, bearing Father's left hand with him. He explained to an awed King Arthur and his court that he had been on the trail of the Questing Beast *(us)* and had just saved a child from its ravening maw when it summoned a demon to attack him. He fought and defeated the demon, but the Questing Beast escaped.

(He was the hero of Camelot for once). Yes, he was. He told us later it was very nice, but he felt a bit guilty for lying. (Honest man). Also, he thought Merlin suspected something, but the magician never voiced any misgivings.

Lancelot *did* point out Pellinore had failed in his original quest *(jealous! Bitter!)* Everyone in Camelot thought that very unsporting and no-one would flirt with him for at least a week (Pellinore said he sulked like a child!) Pellinore was not downcast by his failure to kill the beast, however. He vowed to hunt it for the rest of his life, if needs be.

With Pellinore hunting us, no-one else bothered to and so we got what we most desired – peace *(blissful!)* True, it came at a price. Pellinore made us promise to steal no more sheep from poor people (though he didn't object to our stealing deer off rich men). But we have lived well enough, here in our forest, listening to the birds and the wind in the trees, resting in the shade and swimming in the river.

We saw Pellinore every few years, and he gave us the news from Camelot *(until it fell)*. Yes, Queen Guinevere was beguiled by Lancelot's charm, alluring as dark honey, and everything went to hell **(I told you he was charming!)** Shut up, lion. Though in fairness that spoilt brat Mordred had a hand in its destruction too.

Pellinore survived Camelot's fall, and then his years of kindness towards the peasants and poor people bore fruit. He retired to his family property, a manor house and seven thousand acres, and people flocked to him, to teach him how to manage and farm his land and make it fruitful and prosperous *(and he would give us a whole ox when we visited!)* That was very generous of him. By then he could afford to be generous. He married, and had a clutch of healthy sons and daughters, and died an old, happy man, with his family gathered about him.

(We sneaked in to see him one last time). So we did. He was very ill, but he laughed till he cried when he remembered his everlasting hunt for the Questing Beast, and what had truly transpired. He bade us live a long and content life, and we left. (Pellinore was our friend. We miss him, to this day).

Yes, we miss him. We have watched over his children, and his grandchildren, and great-grandchildren *(Margery's too)*. But we prefer the solitary life these days, and it is easier to attain, the world having relegated us to the pages of a storybook.

We never saw Father again (**there was probably a reason for that**). No matter. He'll be somewhere about his business. Perhaps someday our paths will cross again.

As for us… we have kept our old name, the Questing Beast *(although no-one hunts us these days)*. We feel it suits us. Perhaps someday someone will take up the quest again and try to finish what Sir Pellinore did not (**would not**. Could not).

But we will never have a friend (*opponent?* **Ally?**) as good as Pellinore. History has not been kind to him, but we know better.

Perhaps someday, when King Arthur returns, we might be allowed to return too, and set the record straight.

Brightstar

By Mob

The ravens cawed. Feasted.

We had left them quite the spread.

The Missionary dragged the *vǫlva* up by her collar, knife poised. As the looted houses burned, the "witch" faced the sky, her eyes plucked and unseeing—blackened-dry tears tracked down ruined cheeks, ghost-silver hair bloodied.

In the valleys across from Hitra, we had tracked her to the village among stern granite cliffs and washed them with blood, and let her screams pierce the hearts of the *Ladejarler's* traitors she had dared to harbour. The foreign preacher fumbled with the *vǫlva's* throat, tugging open her shirt at the neck.

Gunnar, my Second, bristled.

I caught him before he could step forward.

"She is already dead."

"*Exactly,*" he spat.

I forced him still, lowering my voice that our men might not hear.

"Think. You would fight one of Grimketel's priests over a foe you helped kill? The King values them enough to bring them over from England."

"The battle is done. That was that. This is this." His muscles strained. The head of his axe twitched. "Do not stop me, *hersir*. We

might trade the old customs for the new, but some Anglo-Saxon
níðingr has no right to play with the dead on our battlefield."

Snick.

Our heads snapped around at the noise. The Missionary stepped
back, a cut leather cord held aloft, and let the *vǫlva's* body fall into the
burning house. Her necklace swayed from his fist. A polished granite
orb hung from it; feldspar veins twisted into the symbol of the
valknut—*Óðinn's* mark winking dull red in the firelight.

"The Lord God is a consuming fire." The Missionary's deep voice
crackled, accent warped. "His flame is Holy Flame."

He flung his hand and *Óðinn's* eye was lost, soaring into the blaze.
The Missionary stepped before the light, arms spread. The older
warriors watched with sneers as he reverently pressed his palms
together, expression sinking to a placid, smiling mask. But I did not. I
looked to our youngest, and watched those same flames flicker on their
eager faces.

There had ever been a cost to strength. More so the strength of a
nation. Of a people. To restore the rightful king, to avoid
power-hungry jarls fracturing our land once again, the old ways could
be no more. The many local faiths would become one, and my king
would grasp this new "church" and its laws.

Yet the more I saw of Grimketel and his priests, the more my
unease grew.

"The Lord is with you," the Missionary said. "He blesses your
blades that His enemies will be destroyed. The witch shall not be
suffered to live. Heretics *will* fall to the lake of hellfire. Their souls

shall not find rest. Where were the village women? Where was the *Ladejarler's* missing gold? Will you not come with me, oh holy warriors, and chase them down for the glory of your King and of your God?"

That bastard. It was not his place. They were mine to command.

In the crowd, youthful vigour outstripped the wisdom of our oldest. I fancied to hear their unvoiced cheers even above the crackling of the timbers, to picture their hunger. A vein pulsed at Gunnar's temple. I motioned for restraint.

The Missionary stood in gore and mud. The burning longhouse framed a halo at his back, its shadows leaving his eyes as holes above that blank smile. I paced to him—sword in hand—waiting for his fear, his retreat. He did not oblige.

I clapped a hand to the man's shoulder, and he finally flinched. An inward grin. I brushed him aside. He would learn his limits, one way or the other.

Past the wreckage, the forest by night was a dark sea outside the village borders—the fires a film of ruddy light against its nearest boughs. The full moon sat at an angle to the lode-star; bright and cold. *Enough for a raid.* The Missionary could report his glory. The men could taste their prize. The deserting remnants of the *Ladejarler's* warriors would face the wrath of our new God.

I raised my blade—raised my voice.

"One veteran per group of five. Five teams enter the forest. Stick to the paths, do not chase blind. Ingvar, stay here with the rest—should any stragglers return, I trust your watch. Get this done and we can return to feast at the great hall in Nidaros." Their shield-roars started as a rumble at my back and grew until they forced me to shout. "In King Óláfr's name, tonight we hunt. No survivors."

"*Ut! Ut! Ut!*" Their cries split into pockets of torchlight as each team charged to the treeline.

Ingvar rounded up the rookies to stand guard over our wagons. Some loaded up the sparse loot, whilst the few with sling-staff or bow took to the shadows and played sentry.

Gunnar came to my elbow, battle-lust in his eyes. "We follow."

It was no question—had not been since we were young ourselves. My grin crept its way out. "Missionary, is that mace of yours for show?"

"Canon law forbids priests to serve as soldiers." Those pitch eyes did not falter. "But I am *permitted* to protect myself."

Bastard. I matched his bland smile with my own. "Then we will just have to put you in danger. Keep up."

****

Bright-star's shine;
battle's bane at battle's end,
be called to gloaming's edge
to walk Hel's path,
and call and call
—a carrion cry across it all—
and howl and weep, and 'last to fall.

****

Dim-silver and dappled yellow-red painted highlights across drifts of slick needles beneath the pines. Split by the trees, the Missionary's torch flickered out stripes of colour. At its edge, a coward of the *Ladejarler's* men edged forward, baring his longknife to the night. Three of his companions followed, the second such party we had met. Their shoulders were tensed—doubtless put to fear that their own footsteps and the soft *crunch-crunch-crunch*ing of those needle-mounds might reveal them too soon.

A mistake.

I signalled Gunnar. We leapt from the rear. A pace to go, I swung my shield. Its boss caught the last of them at his temple as he turned. It struck his hardened leather cap with the noise of shattered bone. He crumpled.

We fell upon the rest. Our battle-cries shook the hearts of those three men stripped of their night-eyes and footing. They spun about, stance disturbed. I took the inside. Ducked. The right's wild jab sailed over my head, his expression confused at no connection, his spear unsteady. My sword slid into his stomach. A jolt. The air filled with rank copper and the stink of spilled guts.

Hot blood sprayed from my left. Half a scream sounded, cut off, lost to the wet gurgle of the spearman. *Gunnar's axework.* Vision sharpened. I wrenched my blade clear, shook off the dying weight. The spearman's body curled—shrimp-like—blubbering pink foam.

Just one lef—

A steel-bright glimmer. *Clang.* I caught the lunge on my shield-rim; slid on the pine needles and compensated, shunting its force outwards. The leader's longknife went wide. He drew a second, stabbing upwards. I swept. Deflected the blow off my crossguard.

Three more strikes. Neck, armpit, groin. No quarter given. My shield chipped, its rim dented. I drew blood from the crook of his elbow. He bared his teeth. Fought on. I matched the snarl. *At last.* A worthy opponent. A veteran in his own right—tired, retreating—eyes flickering to the shadows, gauging escape. Then they widened in shock. Behind, the dull *snap* of gristle and a grunt of satisfaction as Gunnar's axe met some foe.

An opportunity.

I feinted right; a wide slash. He spun—foot stepped out to bring both blades to bear against a heavy blow that didn't come. No chance to adjust on loose needles. My boot met his crotch and his face turned corpse-pale. His knees weakened. I shattered his wrist with the shield's dented rim. One blade fell from a mangled hand. I thrust. He jerked his head aside—futile, desperate—sweat pouring from the hairline.

I closed the distance. Twisted. The return stroke slit his throat.

He sank quietly, his fingers clasping at his neck, the scarlet tide spilling between them all the same. Pupils forest-cat-wide. Lips a silent spasm: *monster*, maybe, curses—lost to the *crunch-crunch-crunching* of those mounds as he lay his last and I stood above him panting gouts of steam. Yet his eyes would not meet my own, gazing off into the distance. I watched him die then checked his pockets.

As we walked back to our torch, I glanced at Gunnar. He shook his head. *No gold, no silver, not even tally-sticks for trade.* From their leader's stash, I turned our dismal prize over and over in the shadows. A triangle of granite, hung from a leather cord. No *valknut* adorned its dull grey faces, just a single word—*blót.* 'Sacrifice.'

Gunnar found three others. He grunted. "No gold."

"No. Just…" Another turn. The rune glinted. Behind, the ravens called, drawn to scavenge our discarded prey.

"Bad omens."

"Yes." Our brows knitted in concert until I broke the silence to hail the waiting bastard. "Missionary. Your work as bait is done. It is time to find the others."

My voice rang between the trees. Those tongues of flickered-yellow-red light answered with uneasy whispers.

"Missionary!" *-issionary, nary, nary.* Naught but echoes returned.

Gunnar glowered. "If his spirit broke and he fled, the forest can keep him."

I barked a laugh, kept crunching footsteps towards the flame. It stole our vision just as it had for the dead. In a short clearing, the abandoned torch sat wedged in curled branches, the oil-fire wavering in too-still air. The Missionary was gone.

To a backdrop of muttered cursing and promises to let wolves gnaw on that bastard's bones, I lifted the torch clear. "Come out. Or we will leave you." *-eave you, you, ou.*

An empty threat. For the sacrifice of the old ways to mean anything, the king's plan had to succeed. The Missionary's polished tongue could not wither yet.

"*Hersir,* look."

Beyond Gunnar's outstretched finger, tendrils of mist curled to the north, spectral in the lode-star's cold shine.

I groaned. "Poor conditions or not, we cannot lose the bastard, no matter how deserved."

His arm did not drop. Tendons stood taught from the skin. Gunnar's spare hand crept toward his axe.

I peered into the mists—no, *fog*, for it thickened farther in, a bank of cloud swamping lines-of-sight in greyed felt—and glimpsed a silver gleam in the depths.

My heart clenched; woozy as sea-legs on land. "Missionary?" *-issionary, nary, nary?*

"Captain… You need to come… Quick…" *-ome quick, wick, ick.* The Missionary's voice twisted between the trees—reed-thin, hissing, barely heard—and faded.

Another flash of silver. Hints of ghostly hair flicked out of sight. Then laughter; bright and clear and cold as the stars above. It did not echo.

A clarion of recognition blared in my mind.

My lips moved, words dripping out to spite my tongue. "That cannot have been her. It is impossible. She is already dead."

"Exactly." Gunnar's grip tightened on the haft of his axe.

"We follow."

Weapons drawn; dark trees swallowed us whole.

****

I call them to me
—murdered, muted—
tongueless rage to turn
from wights' waking wails;
I offer them to Óðinn's sight,
to the raven god's delight,
beneath his watchers' passless might.

****

The fog billowed; shapes garish and floating and then gone as we turned to look. The moon and the stars left luminous channels, tumbling and dusky, disrupting outlines and leaving a vision of negatives. They left us lost in details and turned by snatches of silver hair and cold laughter, feet slipping and crunching and leading themselves by gradient from the path until the tickle and smart of ferns bristled at our intrusion.

"Captain… You need to come… Quick…" *-ome quick, wick, ick.*

It haunted us. Repeating and blending. Neither near nor far, that just-at-the-ear voice distorted—stripped of human touch and foreign tongue and left to hook us and draw us in. We followed. One warrior with two heads, words forgotten, lost in training long-since ingrained as instinct.

We snapped to sudden bursts of sound: the scream of ravens—not yet left behind with their corpse-treats despite our passage; a flutter of silence, endless as the depths of *Rán*; sudden whispers—their direction lost. Once, a wolf howled without answer and we bared our blades and waited for the pack until that bastard's voice echoed in from our front once more.

"How far?" Gunnar held his words level.

I had no answer. We trekked north.

Where was Slørdalsvatnet? Why had we not reached its shores? My questions spiralled. I tamped them down—buried them beneath the next cry of ravens and choked their embers. Stories of the *vǫlva* slid, unbidden, from memory. Their 'magic' had never saved my comrades. Never won a battle. And yet I couldn't banish the nagging of childhood warnings, of the elden forests' dark. I sheathed my sword and held the torch as a totem, our pocket of light small against a vastness without end.

A beat of wings. A burst of black, darker than the dappled fog.

I spun, thrusting out our light, and smote shadows that flowed back at the margins. Tension clamped my spine. My heartbeat squatted in my neck. Gunnar spun with me, axe ready, back to back, covering weakness.

"The mist has thinned." I had to believe it. "I saw their wings."

He shrugged. "Their cawing is louder."

"Closer?"

"Louder."

Unease swirled. *Distance. Time.* Everything was slipping. I glanced at the torch, its flame unchanged despite the passage of night, despite our path, its pitch still smouldering on. I blinked. Coloured shapes skittered across the banks, layers on layers, hypnotic against the fog and the cries of birds.

"Captain…" -*aptain, tain, ain.* That bastard's voice cut through the squall, lost again as the screeching reached new heights.

The clouds swirled. Trailing after his echo, a wind rose, scooping needles, scattering them through the beams of light. Silhouettes joined. Blurry. Half-seen phantoms, wings and feathers. Their quills hid among the needles and streams of brightness; a storm of ravens in the forest, fluttering, their paths unclear. My skin crawled.

One emerged. Greater than the rest. Its shade grew. Larger, defined, edges distinct.

"Gunnar, back!" No time. No swing or bash. I placed my shield as the cloud bulged and something thrust through.

Claws.

Jet black. Inches long. Every scale beetle-bright, jagged, overlapping. The moon vanished, sky darkened, hidden by a wingspan that would not breach the surface of the mists. A beast lurked behind, impossibly large.

There was no sound.

Noise cut out, stolen by a force that showered vision in chipped wood and pressure-bruised colours. Then I was airborne, the torch flying from my grasp.

An impact at my back. A dull grunt. "*Hersir,*" sounded, knocked free from a winded chest. *Gunnar.* Had he tried to catch me? Fool.

Tangled limbs, black sky, dark trees, striped silver, cold light, colder laughter.

We tumbled. Bruises on bruises; ferns bristling and branches biting, head-over-heels, armour worthless; a few metres, it had to stop soon. I tried to tuck in, to restrain arms and legs and resist the next bounce.

It failed to come. My stomach hollowed. In darkness and warped sound, senses muted by the forest, the ground disappeared.

I fell; down and down. Greyness faded, mist thinned, replaced by the black and white of night. A tree. Burst bark and smeared lichen. It split us apart—to spin once more. Through needles and wet, cold mud. At last, I merely rolled. Then the pain came.

Muscles spasmed. I tried to howl and choked out a groan; spat blood at the forest floor where it splashed.

I lay on my side, my left arm still bound to my shield's remains. Cold sweat. Shakes. My thoughts still spun down that hillside in the dark. Above gasped breath, silence gnawed on my ears; the ravens' absence as unnerving as their sudden attack.

Time trickled past. *Seconds? Minutes? Hours?* Mud clung to me. I rolled to all fours. My wrist burned like white-hot lead in place of blood. I scrabbled with the ruined leather shield-strap, shedding fragments of wood and bent iron, pale under the moon like bergfrue petals scattered in spring. The joint throbbed. I cradled it, staggering to my feet.

"Gunnar?" I hissed; fearing an echo, an answer in cackled laughter and sudden claws.

Pain sharpened my sight, sharpened tree branches to knife-limbs. Their edges dripped moonlight. Another stab of agony. I doubled over, moaning at my wrist. A wash of yellow-red light tinted the needle-drifts at my feet, rippling on their outline, torchlight-soft. *Had it followed us down the drop? Was it still lit?*

I squinted for rough bearings. The hillside stretched above to the left, too steep to climb without the guidance of day. To the right, firelight flickered, and yet as I took hesitant paces, I could not approach. No. *Should not* approach. There was no crackle of timbers. No warmth from the flame. No comfort. Just a mocking lure I knew all too well.

I walked the line of light and dark, picking through the moss and the runnels between the ferns. I spotted Gunnar's axe first. The glint of its blade shone through the mud. I hefted it in my good hand and carried on, hesitant and careful and not voicing the worst.

Gunnar lay heaped not twelve paces later. I whispered his name. No response. I leaned in, placed a hand and felt the slight rise and fall of his chest beneath the mail. I traced the helmet until I found a dent and cursed.

Two shakes did nothing. The third produced a soft groan. At the fourth, he opened his eyes and swiped a hand at my throat.

I lifted a finger to my lips. He released his grip, glowered, and clutched his helmet until I thrust the axe into his hands. Then we were up and staring at that uncanny, comfortless light.

"*Hersir,*" he whispered, "that was *Huginn* or *Muninn*. No doubt—"

"We don't know that."

"—*No doubt in my mind.* Have you ever seen a raven like that? *Hersir,* we should retreat."

My jaw clenched. He was right, monster of myth or not. I had no faith in recovering the Missionary. But… "Can you find your way back?"

His pause gave no answer. In its place, noise returned, a faint whispering of branches and needles and insidious breeze that only served to highlight what had been missing. We could not retreat. The forest beckoned.

I drew my sword, made my peace, and let my bad arm swing uselessly at my side. We approached.

At the precipice of colour, the air changed—damp and chill. We wore the fog as a trailing cape. It flowed alongside us; a two-tone breeze, in and out, the bellows-draw of silvan lungs. We did not turn, crossing the threshold of a narrow glade. The smell hit first, as though waiting for us to step inside its jaws before unleashing its stench.

We had stalked battlefields. Roved drunk through slaughter. Combed ash and fragments for trinkets and gold.

That was that. This was this.

Bundled torches ringed the edges, their flame devoid of warmth—the idea of light more than its form. Corpses were piled in the centre, tottering and slipping and still weeping blood, pouring down to a great crimson pool at the base. It lapped with foaming wavelets against shores of dead light, half-thickened with writhing clots that caught in its eddies.

Too much. Too many. My gut clenched. Gunnar paused mid-step.

Even if the entire foetid hillock were bodies to the core, there could never be so much blood that the earth itself would tint like wine. It was impossible. The shattered forms of our men, of the enemy, of the villagers, of the women and children we had never seen. Spirit-shaking. Mind-killing.

Our necks craned upwards. Atop the stack, one of the dead towered above its fellows, legs bent and nailed to the pile with rusted iron stakes, its torso forced upright and head lolling to one side. At its back, the flesh was pulled aside, ribs broken outward and lungs withdrawn and sliced and sliced till organ wings spread and fluttered on that in-and-out breeze as though they could still breathe. As though they might yet fly.

We parted; passing each side of the banks, past this deathly lake and its hideous island. Paced the shores with the fog at our backs, stumbling, dream-like, compelled to view that highest figure face to face, to confirm the silent expectation that chewed its way to my heart and scarred its suspicions inside.

The Missionary's face leered down at us. Lips torn. Bloodied bile spilling to his chest. His eyes were plucked and unseeing—blackened-dry tears tracked down ruined cheeks. The ravens cawed. Abrupt. Violent and hungry.

"We should have run," Gunnar murmured.

The fog mounted the heap and took on shape. Moon-silver hair. Dark eyes. The shade of the *vǫlva* stuck her hand through the Missionary's skull and puppetted his tongue.

"Could you have?" she asked, and her laughter shook constellations. The lode-star pierced brilliant white, twisting into the symbol of the *valknut*. *"We could not run from the Ladejarler's men. They could not run from you. Now it is your turn."*

"You're already dead," I said.

"Exactly."

The fog writhed and the cries of the birds peaked, and *they* stepped through. Raven wings grafted to human form, legs ending in gnarled claws, weapons polished bright, beetle-black scales grown in place of armour, great beaked helms unclear junctions of metal and feathers and flesh. Choosers of the slain. The *valkyrja*.

"I make offerings to Óðinn and Frœyja beneath the brightstar. Tonight, a wild hunt," the *vǫlva* smiled, and through her watched a face of such dreadful beauty I fell to my knees. *"No survivors."*

****

Come one come two;
oh, godly pair, I beg a growth
of wildling wings.
I offer spirits and my shell
to Fólkvangr and Valhǫll's shade—
give stone and flame that I may be renewed,

49

that my fate might be reused.

****

We sought gold and blood and honour. We almost found it all.

But there are no victories in *almost*.

We flee a battlefield of quiet valleys across from Hitra, and yet of lands much further from home. On *Sleipnir's* broad back, a couple of power and beauty and wisdom—so intense our minds burn at the sight—hunt us as we run. A chase of spirits on ravens' wings, and a girl with moon-silver hair and darkened eyes.

We sing a song of screams. A song of precipices and great falls. A song of fangs and sharp beaks and the kiss of death like *jǫtnar's* breath on our necks beneath the famished pile and still we howl to the dark and empty forest.

We leave a fire that is not ours. A holy fire that burns on in an empty village and in the eyes of arrogant youth. It will spread still. Spread until our brothers are buried ash and there are no more warriors to fill those godly halls. The great wolf's jaws may reach us at our end and the world serpent may devour all, but it is not their hunger that swallows the North this night. Tonight, *Miðgarðr* eats its own.

I fly now with my brother and the silver-haired *valkyrja* who chose us to die. To battlefields unending. Until the embers of the world below.

Under a bright star, these are not our flames, yet our homeland catches light.

And there will be no survivors.

Printed in Great Britain
by Amazon

85184628R00030